THE BILLY GOATS GRUFF
AND THE TROLL

Retold by Rose Lewis
Illustrations by Michael Chesworth

PIONEER VALLEY EDUCATIONAL PRESS, INC.

The three billy goats Gruff were hungry.

"This field has no grass," said the big billy goat Gruff. "Let's go over the bridge and get some green grass to eat."

The little billy goat Gruff
went over the bridge.

Trip-trap, trip-trap, trip-trap went his feet on the bridge.

A troll lived under the bridge.
"Who's that going over my bridge?"
roared the troll.

"It is me,
the little billy goat Gruff,"
said the little billy goat Gruff.

"I'm going to gobble you up!"
said the troll.

"Oh, no, I'm too little to eat."
said the little billy goat Gruff.
"Eat my brother. He is bigger!"

And the troll let him go.

The middle billy goat Gruff
went over the bridge.
Trip-trap, trip-trap, trip-trap
went his feet on the bridge.

"Who's that going over my bridge?"
roared the troll.

"It is me,
the middle billy goat Gruff,"
said the middle billy goat Gruff.

"I'm going to gobble you up!"
said the troll.

"Oh, no, I'm too little to eat."
said the middle billy goat Gruff.
"Eat my brother. He is bigger!"

And the troll let him go.

The big billy goat Gruff
went over the bridge.
Trip-trap, trip-trap, trip-trap
went his feet on the bridge.

"Who's that going over my bridge?"
roared the troll.

"It is me, the big billy goat Gruff,"
said the big billy goat Gruff.

The troll jumped up
onto the bridge.
"I'm going to gobble you up!"
roared the troll.

"Oh, no,"
said the big billy goat Gruff.
"You will not gobble me up."

And the big billy goat Gruff
went over the bridge to the field
to eat the green grass
with his two brothers.